MAN ON THE TIGHT ROPE

MAN
ON THE
TIGHT ROPE

by

NEIL PATERSON

Illustrations by Martin Kaye

HODDER & STOUGHTON

The characters in this story are entirely imaginary
and bear no relation to any living person.

FIRST PRINTED 1953

MADE AND PRINTED IN GREAT BRITAIN FOR
HODDER AND STOUGHTON LTD., LONDON, BY
HAZELL, WATSON AND VINEY LTD., AYLESBURY AND LONDON

This story is dedicated to Jaroslav Drobny; to the driver of a certain railway train; and to the many unknown Czechoslovak men and women who, at great risk to themselves and their families, have done a *cernik*.

I

ON THE 15TH OF AUGUST, AT ABOUT
10 a.m., a big black Renault tourer with a
Prague registration number appeared in the
sharp angle of the hills, one of which belongs to
Czechoslovakia and the other to Austria. The car
slid down the cleavage between the hills like a slug
on a woman's bosom, and came to a halt in the
cobbled village square, close by the clock. One of
the two sharp-faced men who occupied the back seat
stepped out and, speaking authoritatively although
in Slovak, demanded to be directed to the circus.
The first two people to whom he spoke appeared not
to understand, but the third, lacking the wit to
comprehend that this sharp-faced man was an agent
of the security police, politely raised his hat and gave
precise directions.

The Circus Cernik was deployed, half a kilometre
to the east of the village, on a flat field of about three
acres—a green peninsula, captured by a shapely loop
of the river, sharply isolated from its neighbours and
dramatised by its boundaries of running water: a per-
fect tober. The Big Top had just been erected; tent-
men were testing and tightening the guys. Caravans,

9

trailers, lorries, buses, all in crimson and gold, stood in the lee of the tent by a line of sycamore trees. Ponies grazed under the shelter of their leaves. Men in shirt-sleeves worked at the shackles of the trailers, unloaded the lorries, shouldered planks and poles, spread canvas on the grass. Women, busy with clothes and buckets, moved in methodical haste to and from the open doors of the living-vehicles. Village children, officious and shrill, fussed around men, women, horses, caravans, and tent; encircled an elephant; importantly helped lift down seat brackets and fork hay for the fodder heap. And all this activity was accompanied by the voice of the circus: the daily cacophony compounded of men's authoritative shouts and unfamiliar animal noises, and the clang of steel hammers and music from half a dozen radios and the occasional revving of engines, and, permeating all the workaday sounds, the high-flying cries of the children.

The Renault tourer nosed across the grass to the encampment. The chauffeur, dressed like the others in dark city-cut civilian clothes, stopped the car and switched off the ignition, and the two hard-faced men got out and walked with unhurried, decisive steps across the tober.

Cernik himself opened the door of his caravan to

them. He was a man of rather less than medium height, of a deceptively slight build, with a thin, brown face in which the chin was prominent, shrewd brown eyes, and brown wavy hair. He wore a ragged khaki shirt and grey corduroy trousers supported by braces of string. He did not look like the owner of a circus. He did not look like the owner of anything.

"You Cernik, proprietor this circus?"

The little man nodded, eyes alert. A wallet appeared in the hands of one of the policemen. There was a flash of papers—credentials: the official photograph, the government stamp.

"Wanted in Brno. Chief of Police."

"Who is it, Cernik?" a woman's voice called from the interior of the caravan.

"Police."

"Crucifix," the woman said. "What do they want now? I thought we'd been through everything with the police."

"These are security police," Cernik said. He watched them intently, noting the inevitable interest in their eyes as his young wife came to the door and leaned her magnificent body against the lintel.

"They want me to go to Brno, Mama," Cernik said. "The Chief of Police wants to see me."

"You can't go to Brno," the blonde girl said,

"you'd miss the matinée. And, besides," she said to the men, "he's been up all night. We just got in. Where'd we come from, Cernik?"

"Vodperk."

"That's right, we just got in from Vodperk. He's been up all night. He has to get his sleep some time, hasn't he?"

"He can sleep in the car."

"Now listen, you——"

"Save your breath, Mama," Cernik said. "You heard what they said. You know I've got to go."

"You!" Mama said. "All of you." Her breasts came up, and she flicked her head, swishing her tawny hair. "You make me sick, all of you. You, Cernik——"

"Now, Mama——"

"Don't Mama me!" The others were forgotten. Her eyes blazed at Cernik, the vulnerable one, the habitual target. "You little squirt, you mild milk-and-water yessing little squirt of a man. Why don't you ever stand up for yourself? My God, call yourself a man——"

"That's enough, Mama."

"I seen better men in a flea-pit. So they want you in Brno! If you were half of half a man——"

"That's enough, Mama," Cernik said sharply.

"Go and make coffee. I'll need coffee. Go and make it."

She was immediately confused. She pushed out her breasts still farther in what was now only a caricature of temper, and then, with a look at her husband which was intended to convey that this was entirely her own idea, she turned sharply and flounced out of sight into the caravan.

The men stood looking at each other.

"She's a hot one all right," the younger policeman said admiringly. "Tell me, brother, is she always like that?"

"She's tired," Cernik said. He drew his hand over the stubble of his chin. He was tired too. Tired and momentarily dispirited. His mind was unwary, it was with Mama and not with the police. He knew that she had come to the door to defend him, and then she had lost the place in her argument and, as a matter of course, had attacked him. It had all happened often before, and it would happen often again. He felt no bitterness, only a great tiredness of mind and of body. "She was up all night," he said. "We had a break-down in the forest. Back axle. Took us three hours to get on the road again." And then he became aware of the policemen as policemen. "I'll need to shave," he said, "clean up." He waited for their comment,

14

but they said nothing, so he set the door in motion. "I won't be long," he said.

Inside the caravan Mama lay in an uncomfortable pose on the bed, face down, ignoring him so consciously that he almost smiled. The kettle was on for his shaving water and there was milk in the coffee-pan. He took off his shirt and singlet, flexed his shoulders. He was a bigger man without his clothes. He had a deep chest, and the strong sloping shoulders that go with it. There was no fat anywhere on his body. One of his arms—the left—was noticeably shorter than the other. Both biceps were flat and corded, the blood-vessels prominent, and the result was that the arms looked older than the body to which they belonged.

Cernik washed to the waist, then shaved, using an old-fashioned cut-throat razor, his movements precise and economical. He put on a clean singlet, ladled coffee into the pan and turned the boiling milk over it. He poured two large cups.

"Coffee, Mama."

She paid no attention. He drank his coffee, watching her, frowning, his mind divided between her and the policemen: twin anxieties.

"Drink your coffee, Mama," he said at last. "It's getting cold."

She still ignored him. He shrugged his shoulders and turned to the let-in wardrobe. He dressed quickly in his formal clothes—a cream shirt, a navy suit, a checked silk muffler folded over at the throat, and, finally, a greatcoat down to his ankles and an American-type hat, tilted far back and worn on his hair rather than on his head.

"I'll be back in time for the evening show, Mama," he said. "They'll manage the matinée all right. Jaro'll take over the clowning routine on the rope, and Fedor and Fedora can double up and Konradin can spin out the shooting stuff." He felt her listening. "I know you're tired," he said placatingly. "Ma Bratislav'll help you with the tickets, and Cara will help too. Where is Cara?"

Caralita was his daughter by his first wife. She was seventeen years old, the apple of his eye.

"Mama. Where's Cara?"

"She went to the village," Mama said without moving.

"What for?"

"Shopping."

"Alone?"

"How would I know?" Mama said. "Cernik," she said, still face down, "I'm sick of it. Police, police, police. Every time you open the door, it's the police.

What do they think we are, anyway? If you weren't such a mouse of a man you wouldn't stand for it. It's that old French bitch to blame. If you would only sack her——"

"Now, Mama, you know I couldn't do that."

"I don't know anything. All I seem to know is that you make me sicker and sicker and sicker."

"You're tired, Mama. Why don't you sleep till dinner-time? You could have your dinner with the Frascatellis——"

"Sleep!" she said into the pillow. "He says, sleep! And all I have to do!"

"Well," he said, beaten, "I'll have to be going. I'll be back as soon as they'll let me. So long, Mama."

She did not reply, and he made a tired little gesture and turned away. But as he reached the door she said, "Cernik," and he saw that she had turned on her back and was regarding him with a warm and brilliant smile. "Take care of yourself," she said softly.

Cernik went out, closing the door carefully behind him. The police agents were standing as he had left them, one on each side of the door of the caravan, and as he went down the steps to join them he saw that the people of the circus had formed an encircling ring. Konradin, sitting on the steps of the caravan opposite

cleaning a ·30 rifle, arched his eyebrows in mute enquiry, and Cernik's lips quirked in a little deprecating smile.

There were people gathered at the doors of the surrounding caravans—Victor Bratislav, ring-master, and Kalina, wardrobe mistress; Rudolph, the tamer; Jaromir the clown, and his wife, Cernik's sister Vina; Vendini, the juggler; Kubelik, the strong-man, who had charge of the apes; Mme la Comtesse, equestrienne; Señor and Señora Frascatelli, equilibrists; Fedor and Fedora, the acrobats; Kaka, the dwarf; Zamek, gaffer of the tent-men. Cernik saw that they were all there, all except—and he felt the usual spirt of irritation—all except Foster, the American—and although they all appeared to be occupied with tasks of one kind or another Cernik knew that they had gathered deliberately, and that they were waiting for him to speak.

"Victor," he said to Bratislav, "you will have to manage the matinée without me. Jaro will fill in for me, and the rest can overlap their times. Fix it anyhow you like. How's your sick cat, Rudolph? Travel all right?"

"Still sick," Rudolph said in his deep guttural voice. "Sick in the belly. It is a dysentery, I think."

Bratislav said, "You will be back for the evening, Cernik?"

"Undoubtedly. I am going only to Brno."

Jaromir the clown, Cernik's brother-in-law and closest friend, said quietly, "You are going of your own free will, Cernik?"

"But of course."

He got into the car, tilted his hat forward, leaned back against the cool leather upholstery, and closed his eyes. The policemen climbed in at each side of him, and the car moved off.

"How long to Brno?" he asked.

"Two hours."

He looked at his watch. 11.35. Two hours. 13.35. An hour's waiting at the police-station and an hour's interrogation. 15.35. Two hours back to the circus. 17.35. Say 18.00. If all went well he would make the evening performance comfortably. *If all went well.*

As they rounded the bend into the main village street the driver said something sharply and jammed on the brakes. A flock of sheep, wedged into the street, advanced on the car, isolated it, slowly jostled past.

"Wait!" Cernik said. "My daughter." He leaned forward, opened the near door, and called, "Cara!"

She didn't hear him. She was standing in the doorway of the provision store talking to Foster, the American. She was looking up into his face, laughing, teasing him, characteristically gay; and the foreigner, equally characteristically, was smiling back at her, with that puzzled, rueful look that emphasised his foreignness. Cernik felt a sharp stab of anxiety. Although he disliked raising his voice, he called her name loudly. "Cara!"

She saw him immediately, immediately absorbed the significance of car and men. Was it his imagination, or was there for one unguarded moment a flicker of guilt in her eyes? He cut off the thought as she darted towards the car: he was too ready to harbour such thoughts.

"Police, Papa?" Cara said. It was not really a question. She wrinkled her nose in disgust. "Where are they taking you this time?"

"Brno."

"What for?"

"Oh, just some routine thing."

"It'll be all right, then, won't it, Papa?"

"Yes, Cara, it'll be all right." Out of the corner of his eye he was aware of Foster watching them, watching and waiting. He can afford to wait, he thought, and felt a heavy and hopeless irritation.

"You'll miss the matinée, Papa."

23

"Yes. But I'll be back for the evening show."

"Will you have time to do any shopping?"

"I don't know."

"If you have time, Papa, could you get me some blue silk? Royal blue. Three metres. And I know that Ma Bratislav wants lace for curtains."

"I doubt if I shall have time," Cernik said. He was still thinking of Foster. "But I shall try. Are you going straight home now, Cara?"

"We are going to have a *café crème* first."

The 'we' stung him.

"Go straight home," he said. "Mama's tired. You ought to be at home helping her." He had spoken with unnecessary sharpness. He tried to make amends. "I'm worried about Mama," he said. "She's tired, overwrought." He smiled deliberately. "Go home and help her, Cara. See to the tickets——"

"Oh, Papa, I'll go home right away, I'll run. I'll look after Mama—everything—for you." She thrust her thin body impulsively into the interior of the car, kissed him on the lips. "And you'll be home soon, Papa?"

"Soon," he said.

When she straightened up, one of the policemen slammed the door. The car moved off. Cernik stared straight ahead until they had left the village far behind, and then he glanced at first one and then the other of the police agents. They were both sitting upright, and on both faces was the curious withdrawn expression that he had noted before on the faces of security policemen. He cleared his throat. "What does the Chief want me for?"

"You'll find out."

"I suppose that means you don't know."

"He thinks we don't know," said the man who had spoken first, and the other man smiled meaningly.

Cernik was not impressed. He knew that this was not an arrest, for if these men had been sent to arrest him they would never have dared to let him dress behind a closed door.

"You boys come from Prague?" he asked.

"Could be."

"Do a lot of this sort of thing, travelling around the country?"

"Fair bit."

Cernik sighed and dived into the pocket of his enormous greatcoat. He offered his cigarette-case.

"Smoke?"

"No."

"How about you?"

"No."

Cernik sighed again, lighted a cigarette, and contemplated the roof lining. He liked to talk at any time, and he would particularly have liked to talk just now. He would have liked to talk the tightness out of his stomach; he craved the comfort of words.

He blew a smoke-ring, and sent another through it and another through that. No dice. The policemen weren't interested in parlour tricks. There was nothing for it but to think. Not that thinking ever helped. "It worries me to see you thinking so much," Jaro had said. "You have a plan. Your plan is to take the entire circus out of the country into free Austria. It is an absurd plan, but it is also a sound plan. It is already sound in every detail, so stop thinking about it. Thinking only gives you a pain in the guts. You show me a good thoughtful clown, and I will show you a disease of the duodenum." And Jaro was quite right, except that Jaro himself was a good thoughtful clown and a fat and happy man, and as far as any-body knew had no disease of the duodenum or any other part of his anatomy. If he had to think, he would like to think happy thoughts about Jaro, but it was not a matter of choice, his thoughts were already decided for him. They were of Cara, and Mama, and the interview with the Chief of Police, and they were all unhappy thoughts.

One way or other it had been a bad season for

Mama, and he wished it was over and he could get her settled in winter quarters, away from all the tension of tenting life, away—let him face it bluntly—away from Rudolph and his accursed cats.

He didn't blame Mama. He was always saying to himself that he didn't blame Mama. He said it so often that he sometimes wondered if it was quite true. But he *didn't* blame Mama. Mama was as she was, and blame was neither here nor there and never could be. How could Mama absorb the wisdom of the circus? She was a city girl and her mind moved in city ways, and as for her glands, they were the work of God. Cernik closed his eyes and looked at the picture of Mama as he had last seen her, lying on her back on the divan, hair splashed over the pillow, eyes big and female, a knee pushed up through the split of her kimono. He didn't blame Mama, but he did sometimes wish that she wasn't quite so crude. She lay in his recollection just like the women in the pictures in the magazines that Kaka the dwarf was always reading. He felt the familiar throb of a little lascivious pulse above his left eye. Mama knew what she was doing. Crude maybe, but effective—*cruci*, how effective!

And immediately he thought of Rudolph, and his stomach ached with anxiety.

28

He reminded himself that Rudolph was a man of honour, and took some consolation from the thought. It was, he reflected wryly, because Rudolph was a man of honour that he disliked him more—far more— than he had disliked any of the others. He disliked Rudolph exceedingly for his sense of honour, yet took comfort in it. What a paradoxical creature a human being was, even an entirely reasonable human being like himself! What a tinker's bag of inconsistencies. There was no refuge in these platitudes. He put his hands on his stomach, feeling his jealousy like a physical thing.

Consider it logically, he thought. It's early morning, Mama is tired, and maybe Jaro'll keep an eye on her until Cara gets home; and when Cara gets back she'll look after Mama, it's astonishing the way they get on together, a miracle, I thank God for it. Cara'll look after Mama all right, she always does.

See, he lied to himself, you look at a worry and it dissolves.

There was Cara, too, to think about. Cara and this foreigner Foster. He had to recognise that at seventeen Cara was grown up. He had been recognising it for some months past in words, but it was not yet a fact in his thoughts. He could accept the flat statement that his daughter was a woman, but

that was as far as he would go. He would not contem-
plate the implications.

He wished irritably that he had never taken Foster
on, and could not understand why he had. Foster had
attached himself to the circus in Kraliky, or was it
Krnov—anyway, it was during the early summer in
Northern Moravia. He had simply adopted the circus
as his home. He lived and travelled with the horses.
He was inoffensive and unobtrusive, and no one,
least of all Cernik, paid attention to him. Then it
began to be noticed that he had a way with horses.
He had natural hands. The Liberties looked better
than ever before; the ponies' coats had an unfamiliar
sheen. At Studenka, Ziska the rosin-back became
sick of the palsy, and the vet. whom Cernik sum-
moned from Vitkovice found her belly full of horse-
bane and gave her forty-eight hours to live. Foster
treated her, cured her. It was then that Cernik became aware of him, and he was amused to learn that
the boy had been with the circus for some weeks. "It
appears to be unnecessary to put him on the pay-
roll," he said. But he had taken him on till the end of
the summer as 'horseman to help with tents.' It had
been a grave mistake. Admittedly Foster was good
with horses, but what did the horses matter when held
in the balance against his daughter's future? . . .

And then there was the overall worry of the plan, and, more immediately, this interview with the Chief of Police. What could the Chief want to see him about? "It's that old French bitch," Mama had said. Well, he hoped so, he hoped it was only that. His mind ranged uneasily over the possibilities, returned to Mama, to Cara, back to the Chief of Police.

Oh well, there was no sense in worrying. No point in thinking. He had been over all this a hundred times, and it had never got him anywhere. What would be, would be. Jaro was right. Thinking was bad for a man. He stubbed his cigarette, leaned back between the policemen, and burrowed almost out of sight into his greatcoat.

In a few minutes he was asleep.

2

CERNIK WAS AWAKE BEFORE THE CAR stopped, but he allowed the policemen to think that they had wakened him. He got out, his coat trailing, and stumped between his escorts up the steps, into the police-station.

It was a modern station, built in the booming years between the wars. The outer office was a large airy room. The walls were painted a dainty pink and decorated with angular blue-print-like paintings of the Town Hall and the University and the Spelberk and the Cathedral of SS. Peter and Paul. There were flowers everywhere—on the window ledges, on filing cabinets, and on the desk. The desk ran the whole length of the room, and behind the desk, at regular intervals, sat five uniformed policemen. And behind them, in the desked-off area of the room, several more policemen sat at little tables, on each of which was a vase of flowers.

His escorts marched Cernik up to the middle-aged policeman who sat in the central position at the long desk.

"This is Cernik," one of them said.

"Cernik. So?" said the man behind the desk, and he laid down his pen and glanced at a convenient sheet of paper. "Jan Cernik?"

"That's me," Cernik said.

The man behind the desk picked up the telephone at his elbow. "My compliments, Chief," he said. "Cernik." He listened, replaced the receiver. "Chief'll see him in half an hour," he announced.

"In that case," Cernik said, "I think I shall do some shopping."

"I wouldn't," the man at the desk said.

"Why not? Am I under arrest?"

"I wouldn't say exactly that you are under arrest, Circus Proprietor Cernik. Not exactly. I merely offer you my official advice. In my opinion it would not be wise for you to leave."

Cernik looked from face to face. He felt anger rise in him, and cut it off with an effort of will. They have faces like machines, he thought. They have turned their machine-like faces on me to intimidate me. He shoved his hands deep into the pockets of his coat, and nipped the material of the linings between thumbs and forefingers. He concentrated all his strength in his fingers. "Nice place you have here," he said mildly. He sauntered to the nearest window and looked out. He could see only a graveyard with a high wall, and, above the wall, tenement roofs and a distant factory chimney. "Nice view."

No one answered him. He sat down on a bench by the wall and pulled out his cigarette-case.

"It is forbidden to smoke," the man at the desk said.

Cernik began to sweat. He put his cigarettes back in his pocket, tilted his hat forward so that his face was concealed, crossed his feet, and leaned back against the wall.

"I regret about the smoking," the man at the desk said. "But you will understand it is bad for the flowers."

Cernik did not reply. He breathed deeply and regularly. He hoped he was presenting a convincing picture of a man falling asleep. But this time he was very wide awake.

Later—much later—he was taken behind the desk to the office of the Chief of Police.

The Chief was a small man, smaller and slighter then Cernik, with a large close-shaven head and enormous, dark, luminous eyes. He wore a navy tunic with epaulettes, and Cernik felt that if it had not been for the epaulettes his head would have been as wide as his shoulders. He sat at a massive leather-covered

desk built on pedestals of drawers. On the wall behind him were two huge maps of Brno and o.
Moravia. There were no flowers in the room.

The two security policemen brought Cernik up to
the desk, and the Chief acknowledged them with a
little dip of his head and at the same time crossed
and uncrossed his hands in a colourful gesture of dis-
missal.

"Your papers, if you please."

Cernik handed them across.

"Now that we are alone," the Chief of Police said,
"you may sit down. These security chaps like things
done in a very formal way. Sit down and make yourself comfortable, Circus Proprietor Cernik. Have a
cigar."

"I shall smoke a cigarette, if I may."

"By all means. Well now, our business." He
opened a folder and began to recite briskly. "You are
Jan Cernik, forty-three years of age, proprietor of the
Circus Cernik. Born 8th March 1908, in the village
of Gran in the province of Silesia, third son of
Wilhelm Cernik, cobbler. Is that correct?"

"Correct," Cernik said.

"You have been associated with circus life since
1918 when you ran away from home to join the
Cirque Africaine as foil for your paternal uncle,

Bernard Cernik, trampoline acrobat. In a fall in the summer of 1920 you sustained an injury to your left arm, and as a result of this injury your left arm is five inches shorter than your right. Be good enough to extend your arms to me . . . thank you. Subsequently, on your discharge from hospital, you joined the Circus Varnsdorf as a tent-boy. There you took up wire-walking, and first appeared in public as a wire-walker in Pilsen in October 1925. There, too, you first became acquainted with the woman who calls herself Mme la Comtesse d'Aragon, equestrienne." The Chief's voice had not changed, but Cernik suspected that he had come to the point. "Is that correct?"

"That is all correct, Chief, save that my uncle Bernard was not a trampoline acrobat, he was a Risley artiste. R-I-S-L-E-Y." He spelled it.

"It is not of consequence," the Chief said, making the alteration. "But I like to have things correct. In 1931, at the age of twenty-three, you opened the Circus Cernik. Where did you get the money?"

"I had some money saved. But most of it came from the National Bank."

"And—I put it to you—from Mme la Comtesse?"

"She advanced me a small sum."

"Why?"

Cernik shrugged his shoulders. "From sentiment, perhaps."

"You were her lover?"

Cernik smiled. "When I first met Mme la Comtesse, Chief, she was in her fifties, an elderly woman, and I was a boy in my teens."

"Nevertheless, one hears of such liaisons."

"I was not her lover," Cernik said.

"Your relationship, then, was rather that of mother and son?"

It was an incongruous idea. "Mme la Comtesse is a woman of some asperity," Cernik said. "I cannot think of her as a mother, Chief, nor can I imagine her entertaining maternal feelings. Our relationship was that of friends."

"So," the Chief said, convinced but puzzled. "Well, to continue. In 1933 you toured not only Southern Bohemia but also the Austrian Tyrol. In September of that year you married. . . . I think we can omit all this . . . daughter born, wife died, married again. Ah yes, here we are. In 1939 you volunteered and were accepted for active service on the Sudeten frontier, although your disability would have freed you from the necessity of taking up arms. Circus Proprietor Cernik, I am instructed to ask you why you volunteered for the Army in 1939."

38

"It seemed necessary," Cernik said.

"I think it only fair to warn you," the Chief said, speaking very slowly and distinctly, "that importance attaches to this point. What were your motives in 1939 in disbanding your circus and joining the Army?"

"I do not recall that I had any particular motives. The Germans were massing on the border. It seemed necessary to be a soldier. It was a matter of obligation."

"Your motives were political?"

Watch it, Cernik said to himself, watch it, here it comes. "I know nothing of politics, Chief. I am a man of the circus."

The Chief sighed. "It is not yet a crime to take an interest in politics. You had strong feelings against the Germans? You are a patriot?"

"I would not claim so much. I regard myself only as a Czech."

"And it was solely for reasons of patriotism that you joined the Army in 1939?"

"I suppose so," Cernik said cautiously. "It seemed necessary at the time."

"Very well," the Chief said, and he made a little mark in the dossier. "That is established. Now, with regard to Mme la Comtesse . . . you will be aware, no doubt, that it is because of this woman that you have been brought before me?"

Cernik sighed openly in relief. "I thought it likely," he said, smiling. "This is not the first time I have been examined. I suppose she has been writing letters again?"

"Many letters. She has also been speaking in shops, in trams and buses, to passers-by in the streets. I have here a detailed record of her latest indiscretions. Is she insane?"

"No," Cernik said. "I would not call her insane."

"Then what is the matter with her?"

"She is of the old brigade," Cernik said, choosing his words carefully. "She does not understand the modern processes of government. She feels strongly."

There was a moment's silence.

"Cernik," the Chief said, "I wish to be frank with you. You are plainly a man of character and intelligence, and I think it is in your best interests, and in mine also, that I should be entirely truthful. My instructions are to frighten you. Instead, I shall merely tell you the truth. Mme la Comtesse is described in this paper before me as a dangerous and seditious person. She has plainly become an embarrassment to the régime. You may ask, as I too have asked myself, why it is that the oblique approach should be made. Why should you, the employer, be held responsible? Why is it that the lady herself is not imprisoned or deported? It is my personal opinion that the answer is to be found in her history. Mme la Comtesse has been, in her day, a very distinguished woman. She is known all over the world—Paris, Berlin, London, Vienna, Constantinople, New York—she has had triumphs everywhere. And she is an old woman. You will have noticed, Circus Proprietor Cernik, that governments everywhere are sensitive to world opinion, and especially new revolutionary governments. Our own masters are no exceptions. They do not wish to incur odium abroad by imprisoning or even deporting this famous old woman, but they are determined to make it impossible for her to remain in Czechoslovakia. And that is why they are putting pressure on you, Cernik; that is why you are sitting here before me today. You have been warned before against this woman, and you have taken no action. Suspicion is now falling on you personally——"

"That is impossible," Cernik said. "I am non-political. I take no sides."

"It may be necessary to take sides," the Chief said mildly. "The official view is that you are in effect condoning the seditious behaviour of this old aristocrat by retaining her at your circus. By the

41

way, is she truly aristocratic? Is the title genuine?'

"I do not know," Cernik said. "I imagine not. But she has used it for so long that she believes in it herself. As for discharging her, she is an old woman, Chief, and the circus is her home. She must be over seventy."

"Seventy-two," the Chief said. "I understand the argument and I condone the sentiment, but you carry both to excess. You do not appear to appreciate your own danger. It is against you officially that you volunteered unnecessarily for the Army in 1939; this marks you as a man of initiative, a man who is prepared to act on his principles. Such men, I regret to say, are regarded as dangerous. You are yourself under suspicion, Circus Proprietor Cernik, as a person who is not politically reliable."

"That is a monstrous allegation, Chief."

"Nowadays," the Chief said calmly, "people are hanged every day on just such monstrous allegations. Allegation is the new form of proof. It must be clear to you from what I have told you that neither you nor anyone else can now help this woman. She is beyond assistance. If you persist in championing her, all you will achieve is your own destruction. You are a sensible man, Circus Proprietor Cernik. Behave sensibly. Get rid of her. Come now, give me an assurance that you will do so immediately."

Cernik said, "I shall consider it carefully, Chief."

"That is not enough," the Chief said. "It is past the time for considering. Hitherto I have spoken as an individual. I have spoken as one who does not owe his promotion to the present régime. It is my duty now to speak to you as an official of the Government. Today is the 15th. I am instructed to inform you that as from today you have precisely one week in which to terminate your association with this woman."

He pressed the bell on his desk. The interview was at an end.

3

IT WAS HALF-PAST SIX IN THE EVENING
when Cernik returned to the circus. He had
taken a train to Znogmo, and, of necessity, a taxi
from Znogmo on, and he had been overcharged. He
was tired and irritated and worried.

Mama was not in the caravan. He stood in the
doorway, his hat on the back of his head, looking
carefully round the interior of his home, searching
deliberately for some clue to Mama's whereabouts and
to the nature of her day. He felt a movement behind
him and turned sharply. It was only Vina, his sister,
Jaro's wife. She was a little wizened woman, not
unlike him, with frizzy hair and brown cautious eyes.
She had just opened the door of her caravan opposite,
and was about to shake out a mat.

"Seen Mama?" he said.

"No," she said. "Cara said she was sleeping. But
that was in the afternoon. How did it go in Brno?"

"Not too bad," he said. "Tell Jaro——" He hesitated. "Tell Jaro I'll want a meeting tonight. Here, in
my place. After the show."

"A meeting?" she said, curious. "A meeting of
who?"

44

His sister knew nothing of the plan. Neither did his wife. Nor his daughter. None of the women knew.

"Just tell Jaro a meeting," he said. "He'll understand. And if you see Mama, tell her I'm back and that I've gone over to Madame's."

He walked round the perimeter of the encampment. His objective was the ornate, old-fashioned trailer-caravan belonging to Mme la Comtesse d'Aragon, but he approached it by a deliberate detour that would take him past the door of Rudolph's caravan.

"I shall not speak to him," he thought.

He threaded a way between caravans and tents and lorries, ducking under guy-ropes and lines of washing, acknowledging greetings with automatic gestures of head and hands. He told himself that he was thinking only of Mme la Comtesse and of the Plan, and that it was entirely natural that his temples should be throbbing and that there should be sweat on the palms of his hands.

He found himself climbing the steps of Rudolph's caravan. If he must speak to Rudolph, he would do so with circumspection. He would merely inform him that there was to be a meeting of the planners tonight, and that was all.

There was no reply to his knock, and he was

sorely tempted to try the door, but would not. As he stood, irresolute, Rudolph came round the side of the caravan and halted at sight of him. They stood eyeing each other like a pair of hostile dogs, the little insig-nificant man engulfed in the greatcoat and the big colourful man in white silk shirt and black breeches. Cernik looked at the florid face and glistening black moustache, and circumspection was forgotten. He said, "Seen Mama?"

Rudolph said, "Not since the afternoon."

Cernik stood waiting.

"She came over in the afternoon."

Cernik still waited.

"I didn't let her in."

Cernik, without taking his eyes off Rudolph, put a cigarette in his mouth, but did not light it.

"She wanted me to fix a lamp, she said——"

"I don't want to know what she wanted," Cernik said. "All I wanted to know was, have you seen Mama?"

"Well," Rudolph said, "I've seen her."

Cernik slowly lighted his cigarette. He blew out a thin projectile of smoke, stepped down to the ground, and turned away.

"Cernik," Rudolph said softly. "Listen to me, keep her away from me."

Cernik stopped in his tracks, but did not turn. He said, "Rudolph, when I want advice from you I'll ask for it."

"Don't try me too hard, Cernik. I have only good-will towards you."

It was true too. The sentimental German *kraut*. He was full of good-will, and there was nothing about him that irritated Cernik more. He smiled and said lightly, "You're a good chap, Rudolph, and I depend on you." And he nodded and walked on.

He felt better, much better, free to give his mind exclusively now to Madame, and Madame's folly and its effect upon the plan. The problems that had weighed so heavily on him only a few seconds before now merely stimulated his imagination. He was no longer the slave of the plan. He was its master. He lengthened his stride and began to whistle tunelessly between his teeth. He had walked fifty yards before he realised that he had forgotten to tell Rudolph that there was to be a meeting that night. . . .

He knocked on the door of Madame's caravan.

"Who is it?" her precise voice demanded.

"It is I—Cernik. I want to see you."

"I am dressing."

He smiled. She was always dressing.

48

"Nevertheless, I want to see you, Madame. It is a matter of importance."

"Nothing is of more importance to me than my toilette."

Cernik waited, mastering his impatience. He knew that she had simply spoken the truth when she had said that nothing was more important than her toilette. It was now her life's work. Her dressing-table and her shelves were crammed with jars and bottles of all shapes and sizes—a veritable armoury of cosmetics—and her wardrobes were packed with contraptions, ingenious to the point of obscenity. She spent the greater part of each day working with an artist's concentration on her wigs, her face, her figure; and the result, when seen under the arc-lights, was entirely effective. The face was a mask of youth, the figure a triumph of engineering, but audiences saw only a youngish and glamorous woman. Everyone in the circus knew how important Madame's toilette was, and no one, least of all Cernik, would have thought of interrupting it without good reason. Madame, also, must know that.

He knocked again, sharply. "Madame!"

"Cernik," Madame said, "I shall receive you when I have completed my toilette, and not before. I shall send for you."

Anger flared in him.

"Very well, be kind enough to listen to me. I have spent the day on your account in the police-station in Brno. You have been indiscreet for the last time. There are to be no more warnings. I have been given precisely one week in which to discharge you."

There was silence. He imagined her busy hands arrested in mid-air.

"Did you hear me?"

"I heard you," she said.

He walked away. There was some sort of commotion in the Big Top, but it did not engage his mind: there were always commotions. Madame was impossible, but he should not have lost his temper. She was an old and celebrated woman, and it was his duty to indulge her; no one else ever did nowadays.

He became aware of his nephew Karel.

The boy was running towards him. "Uncle," he was calling in an unnecessarily loud voice. "Uncle, you're wanted in the Big Top."

"Hullo, Karel," he said easily. He was always easy in an emergency. "What is it? What's the matter?"

"It's Kaka."

"What's that accursed dwarf been doing now?"

"He's up a king-pole and won't come down. He's

got a knife. Fedor went up for him, and Kaka slashed at him."

"Hurt him?"

"No." The boy was a true son of Jaro; his eyes danced with humour. "Just his dignity. He had to slide a couple of metres down the pole like a monkey. We've had a lot of fun, but I think my father's getting worried because they're beginning to line up at the pay-box."

"All right, Karel," Cernik said. "Run on and tell them I'm coming." But first he had something to do. He had a mental picture of Madame's eyes staring from their mask like stricken beasts in a cage. He had been unnecessarily cruel. He turned back quickly, and knocked again on the door of her caravan.

"Yes?"

"It's Cernik again. We'll have a talk later. All I want to say just now is that somehow I shall find a way out of this difficulty. I have no intention of discharging you."

"Naturally not," Madame said, speaking in her most disdainful, aristocratic voice. "Where would this little piss-pot of a circus be without me?"

Cernik turned away towards the Big Top. "The old bitch," he said admiringly. She was utterly impossible. But you had to grant it—she was also magnificent. She wanted no sympathy, and she needed none.

And now for Kaka.

He thrust aside the flap of the Big Top and walked in. There was a crowd round the farther king-pole. Mama—yes, there she was—and Foster and Cara, standing together, and Jaro and Ma Bratislav, and Fedor and Fedora, and Kubelik, and a dozen tent-men, and a host of children. They were all speaking and shouting, and they were all looking up at the top of the king-pole where Kaka the dwarf clung gesticulating and jabbering down at them like an excited monkey.

"What's all this about?" Cernik demanded.

Everybody started to tell him at the same time.

"Shut up," he said. "Jaro?"

"Mustard in the apes' food," Jaro said. "Kubelik chased him into the tent, and he shinned up the pole. Fedor went up after him——"

"He tried to stab me," Fedor said.

"Yes, he did," Fedora said. "See the steel in his hand. The abomination of a pigmy!"

"All right," Cernik said. "All right, I know the rest."

"It's a lie! It's a lie!" Kaka was screaming.

"Let me get my hands on him," Kubelik said. "I

shall tear his joints apart. Let me have him inside these hands, Cernik, for thirty seconds, that is all I ask."

"It's a lie!" Kaka screamed. "It's a conspiracy!"

"Cernik," Mama said, her eyes feverish, "you'll have to thrash him. You will thrash him, won't you?"

"Hush, Mama," Cernik said. "Hush, everybody." He looked up at Kaka, still gesticulating, still screaming, and made up his mind. "Jaro," he said, "clear the tent. Everybody out."

Mama said, "You'll let me stay, Cernik."

"Everybody out," Cernik said. He took a cigarette from his pocket and put it in his mouth.

"All I want is thirty seconds of him only, Cernik," Kubelik said.

"Come on now," Jaro was shouting. "Outside. All of you. Everybody out."

"Cernik," Mama said, gripping his arm. "Take him to the caravan. Do that for me. Take him to the caravan, Cernik."

He looked at her.

"Please, Cernik, please!"

"All right, Mama, you go and make a sandwich. A mustard sandwich. A hot one. And, Mama, I'll want my supper."

54

"It's in the grill," Mama said. "It's all ready for you." She looked up at Kaka. "The little beast," she said in a relish of disgust, and she squeezed Cernik's arm affectionately. "Oh, this is fun, Cernik!"

... The tent was empty now. Kaka jabbered on, protesting his innocence. Cernik paid no attention. He did not even look up. He smoked his cigarette stolidly, apparently unconscious of the little frenzied figure above, and the dwarf's protestations became more and more spasmodic, and finally dwindled away altogether. Cernik dropped his cigarette end and screwed it into the ground with the heel of his shoe.

He said in conversational tones, "Come down, Kaka."

"No," Kaka said. He began to scream again. He hadn't been near the apes. It was Kubelik himself. Kubelik had always hated him. And another thing. He had seen one of the tent men put something in the apes' plate. It was something out of a tube. He couldn't remember the man's name, but he knew him well by sight, and he would point him out to Cernik: he was a bad man, there were a lot of bad men in the circus. Kubelik was a bad man and this tent man was a bad man and there were other bad men, and they were all in a conspiracy against poor

Kaka, the poor innocent little dwarf. He wept in a great gust of self-pity.

Cernik waited till the paroxysm had passed. "Come down, Kaka," he said.

"No, they'll kill me."

"In all the years you have been with me," Cernik said, "have I ever let anyone lay hands on you?"

"Nobody except yourself," Kaka said. "But if I come down you'll thrash me, and last time you thrashed me *you* nearly killed me." He began to cry again.

It was true. He had caught Kaka spying on Mama, and he had been angrier than a man in authority has ever any right to be. He had been angry with Mama for being careless, and he had taken it all out on Kaka and had thrashed him within an inch of his life. He did not like to be reminded of that. He said, "Come down, Kaka, and I shall not thrash you."

"You promise it?"

"I promise it."

"Promise it on the life of your daughter. If you thrash me, may she die in an agony of disease. Swear it, Cernik."

"I swear it," Cernik said.

56

"Say it in the words. I shall not come down unless you say it in the words."

"All right," Cernik said. "If I thrash you, may my daughter die in an agony of disease. Now drop the knife."

Kaka hesitated, then threw the knife to the ground. "Now come down."

Kaka slid down the pole, slowly at first, and then, as he neared the ground, in a sudden rush, but Cernik was prepared for this manœuvre and grabbed him before he could escape.

"Give me your hand, Kaka."

"What are you going to do with me?"

"I would like to do nothing at all," Cernik said. "But you would not understand that, and neither would Kubelik nor the rest of the people. I am going to give you what you gave the apes."

They left the tent hand in hand. Kaka was silent, but as they approached Cernik's caravan he began to whimper. "There was only a very little mustard in their food," he said.

Mama was waiting for them in a state of great excitement. "I've made the sandwich, Cernik," she said. "But I think it would be much better if you thrashed him. It's the only thing he understands."

Cernik's belt was laid out on the table, and along-

57

side it a sandwich. "Thrash him, Cernik," Mama said. She touched the belt. "Go on, Cernik. Give it to him."

"There is to be no thrashing, Mama," Cernik said. He nodded at the sandwich. "Take your medicine, Kaka."

Kaka picked up the sandwich and eyed them over it, his little eyes darting balefully from one to the other.

"If you spit out as much as a mouthful," Cernik said, blocking off the obvious escape, "I shall take the sandwich in my fingers and ram it down your throat inch by inch." And Kaka knew from old ex⁄perience that Cernik, having said this thing, would do it.

"If he won't eat it, you'll beat him, won't you, Cernik?" Mama pleaded.

"He'll eat it," Cernik said. He took no satisfaction from a scene of this kind. On the contrary, he greatly disliked it. It was simply his duty to mete out justice, and he wanted to get it over and done with. "Eat it, Kaka," he said curtly.

The dwarf took a tiny nibble at a corner of the sandwich, and another and another. Finally, a bite.

"More," Cernik said.

As if in temper, the dwarf thrust half the sandwich into his mouth. Tears spurted from his eyes, his face

58

became purple, and he fell to his knees, clawing with both hands at his throat, screaming. "You're murdering me," he screamed. "Oh, mother of God, my neck, my guts! I'll kill you for it, Cernik; kill you, d'ye hear, kill you. Ah God, mother o' God, the hate, the hot agony! . . ."

Cernik opened the door, and with his foot bundled the squirming body of the dwarf towards it. The scene disgusted him, and the dwarf's hatred aroused disturbing echoes in his memory. He was Kaka's protector. He had saved Kaka time without number from the vengeance of his victims. Once or twice he had even saved his life. Yet he knew that the dwarf's only feeling for him was hatred, a genuine burning hatred. Kaka hated nearly everyone, but he hated Cernik more venomously and more consistently than he hated any other living person. And Cernik knew it, and did not understand it, and worried over it.

Kaka had started to curse Mama now, putting his finger with deadly accuracy on Cernik's Achilles' heel. He cursed Mama and Mama's body, and what she did with it and who she did it with. He cursed her and all her female works in one long breath, with detailed and dreadful obscenity.

"Get out!" Cernik said, in a cold rage, and he toed the creature through the door.

Kaka shrieked, there was one last violent obscenity, and then the sound of retching. Cernik slammed the door.

"Lock it," Mama said. "Lock it, Cernik."

She was lying on the divan, her eyes on him, glittering, big and black, her nostrils dilating. "You should have thrashed him, Cernik," she whispered, and he saw that last terrible thrashing in her great eyes. "You should have thrashed him, but it doesn't matter now."

"I shall speak to Kaka later," he said. "He will never say such things again. I shall see to it, Mama."

"Oh, Kaka's all right," she said. "Never mind Kaka. Don't stand there making speeches, now."

He deplored her excitement and the cruelty that had aroused it, and the purging it now demanded. He hated this urgency of hers, yet exulted in it. He was its willing and practised accomplice.

"For God's sake lock the door," she said.

Her lip was up in a sort of snarl. She was ugly when she looked at him like that, challenging him on an animal level, demanding a complementary brutality from him, and, *cruci*, he always had it for her, and to spare. He felt on his face the same ugly expression that he saw on hers.

Without taking his eyes off her, he locked the door.

61

4

THE FOLLOWING MORNING THERE WAS an event unprecedented in the history of the circus.

Heinrich Cheb paid a visit.

Cheb was proprietor of a rival circus. The Circus Cheb and the Circus Cernik were approximately the same size and, since the war, had travelled the same routes. There was bitter enmity between them. Each had bribed the other's advance agents, torn down the other's bills, repeatedly and treacherously queered the other's pitch. Each had a score of genuine grievances against the other, and on the few occasions when the circuses had met there had been open and bloody battle, with heads split open, wagons overturned, and the inevitable sequel of vindictive litigation.

It was Bratislav who brought the news of Cheb's arrival. He was an old and dignified man, but he ran like a boy among the caravans, calling for Cernik. He found him at last under the Ford lorry at work on the back springs, and he was so full of the news that he could not wait till Cernik had crawled out, and himself crawled underneath to impart it.

"Who?" Cernik said, wrenching with a spanner at a nut.

"Cheb," Bratislav repeated.

"Heinrich Cheb?"

"Himself. Believe it or not, Cernik, asking for you. He's at your caravan."

Together they wriggled out from under the lorry.

"Is he alone?" Cernik demanded.

"He has four of his men with him."

Cernik looked at the spanner in his hand. If Cheb were here, it could only mean trouble. He said, "Does Jaro know?"

"Everybody knows. I never saw anything go through the circus so quick. And everybody's watching him. He won't start anything, Cernik. He wouldn't dare."

Cernik dusted himself down and set off across the tober, Bratislav panting at his side.

"What do you think he wants, Cernik?"

"How would I know?" Cernik said curtly. He saw Cheb a long way off, and the hairs on his neck rose like a terrier's.

Cheb was standing by the door of Cernik's caravan, closely surrounded by his bodyguard. There were four of them, and they were all big men, but Cheb towered above them. He was always a remarkable sight. Today he wore a huge sombrero and

63

a frilled Indian coat, and he was smoking the longest cigar that Cernik had ever seen. He was a showman, whereas Cernik was an artiste, and each despised the other on this account.

When Cheb saw Cernik, he took his cigar deliberately from his mouth and spat. Cernik walked right up to Cheb, halting only when his head was under the big man's hat.

"You have a nerve, Cheb," he said.

"I have probably more nerve than any man in the country," Cheb said in his great booming voice, and his eyes twinkled inside their blinkers of fat. "It is generally known."

"What do you want?"

"I came to *parlari*."

Cernik looked around. His people were all there, perplexed, waiting like children for some indication as to how they should behave. He was perplexed too. He fingered the lobe of his ear, looked meaningly at Jaro, and Jaro nodded.

Cheb saw and understood the exchange. He said, "Tell your people not to interfere with my men."

"Your men won't come to any harm as long as they behave themselves," Cernik said. He jerked his thumb at the door of his caravan, and Cheb, after a moment's hesitation, preceded him up the steps.

Mama was standing by the stove, trying to look unconcerned. Cheb swept off his sombrero with a gallant bow. "Mme Cernikova, I believe." But Mama looked only at Cernik. Cernik said, "Outside," and Mama went out like a scalded cat.

Cernik closed the door, and Cheb seated himself in the only chair and looked around, plainly approving Mama's tinselled furnishings. He said, "Nice place you have here. Surprisingly elegant, if you understand me."

Cernik remained standing. "Come to the point, Cheb."

"Last night," Cheb said, "you had a meeting here, in this room. Those present were"—he produced a scrap of paper from the crown of his hat and read—"yourself, Jaro, Bratislav, Conradin, Kubelik, Fedor, Rudolph. Do I interest you, Cernik?"

"Go on speaking," Cernik said.

"I know what you talked about."

Cheb leaned back negligently in the little armchair. On his fresh chubby face, clean-shaven save for tailored tufts of hair on the cheek-bones, there was an expression which was almost benign. Cernik stood bent slightly forward balancing on the balls of his feet, like a fighter on the edge of movement, every muscle in his body tensed for action.

66

"I disbelieve you," he said at last.

"You talked," Cheb said blandly, "about your plan to escape into Austria. You discussed the dates. The original date for the escape was the 1st of September. In view of your visit to Brno yesterday and the warnings given you by the Chief of Police, you, Cernik, were in favour of advancing the date. You also discussed the advisability of telling your womenfolk of the plan and decided against it, and you discussed the identity of the spy who has been informing on the Frenchwoman's stupidities. I believe that you suggested that it might be your young American horseman—I even know why you suggested that, Cernik —but the others pooh-poohed the idea. Do you believe now that I know what you talked about, or do you want to hear more?"

"No more," Cernik said. There were bright red spots on his cheek-bones, and his eyes had become small and narrow and ugly. "Who told you?"

"The dwarf."

"Kaka!"

"Who else? You should treat your employees better, Cernik, or, failing that, secure the floor-boards of your caravan."

Cernik's face was a picture. Cheb read his thoughts

unerringly, and threw back his great head and laughed aloud.

"Violence won't do any good, Cernik. I have made my arrangements. Dead or alive, I hold you in the hollow of my hand."

It was a bitter moment for Cernik.

For three years, ever since the Communists had taken power, he had lived with the plan. It had grown in his mind, as a tree grows from a seed, nurtured day by day by the persecution of his friends, by police interrogations and searches, by the growing bewilderment and unhappiness of his fellow-countrymen, until now it enveloped and possessed him. He had lived with the plan, and he had lived for the plan. He had conceived it as a gesture. To take an entire circus through the Iron Curtain would be an act of superb showmanship. It would be a statement of protest and revolt which would be understood and appreciated all over the world. But the plan had grown until it was now far more than a gesture. It had become an obsession, his dominating aim. He was dedicated to it. His future—and not only his—the future of his family and friends—their very lives—depended on it.

And now a dwarf had told a tale, for spite, and all their dreams were blasted and their lives hung on a thread. And Heinrich Cheb held that thread.

Cernik could see only one slender hope: that somehow he might strike some bargain. He cleared his throat and said, "What do you want, Cheb?"

Cheb said, "Nothing. I merely came to warn you."

Those words were meaningless.

Cernik said, "State your terms, Cheb."

"My dear Cernik, if I may say so, you are an obtuse and ungracious little man. I should like some coffee. And then perhaps you will do me the honour of sitting down and talking to me like a human being. I am here to help you. I'm non-political, but if I were a younger man, damn me, I'd come with you! Do you know their latest? They've actually stopped me doing my Jan Hus parade. Decadent, they say. Jan Hus . . . decadent! By the Lord God, I don't know where it's going to end. . . ."

Cernik listened. His face was expressionless, yielding not the slightest flicker of relief, and Cheb, watching him, thought what a cold, hard, unfeeling little man he was. He could not know that Cernik's heart was fluttering like a captive bird's. "I take it, then," Cernik said quietly, "that you do not intend to inform on me?"

"Certainly not," Cheb said. "I have no liking for you, Cernik, but a matter like this is an apple off another tree. Now can I have some coffee?"

69

Cernik turned to the stove. He lit the gas-jet and put the coffee-pan on. His hands were unsteady.

"The dwarf came over in the middle of the night," Cheb said. "I'm in Trebic, I suppose you know that. He'd thumbed a lift from a lorry. I sent him back, told him to keep his mouth shut, behave as if he knew nothing, and that I'd take him on after you were arrested. If you want my advice, it's this, Cernik. I'd move quick if I were you. If that dwarf knows, anybody may know. You don't want to waste time."

"I think that is good advice," Cernik said. He had accepted the incredible fact that Cheb was friendly, and his mind had moved on from this phenomenon and was already at work on the new problems that immediate escape presented. The plan had depended essentially on timing. Could arrangements be made for tonight? It was all a matter of synchronisation, split-second timing. . . . M'm yes. And meantime . . . there was Cheb. "I shall be leaving the tent, Cheb. I should be pleased if you would accept the tent."

"Is it in good condition?"

"It is almost new."

"In that case I accept the tent," Cheb said. "Have you any plans for the seating?"

"I should be pleased if you would accept the seating also."

"What about the elephants?"

"I am taking the elephants."

"What of the rest of the animals, then?"

"You could have the wolves," Cernik said. "But you will have to collect them. We shall be freeing the wolves in order to create a diversion. I am taking everything else with me."

"The tent, the seating, and the wolves," Cheb said. "It is not as much as I had hoped for."

"When I am gone," Cernik said, "you will have a clear field."

"That had not escaped me."

"And the tent is in very good condition. You can also have the king-pole wagon. I had forgotten about the wagon." As he spoke he had been thinking with that brilliant clarity that sometimes illumines the mind in moments of crisis. He saw his course clearly. He saw the entire pattern of events that he must presently devise, and in that complicated pattern he saw a place, and a use, for Cheb. "Listen, Cheb," he said. "This is how I'm going to do it."

"First, the coffee," Cheb said.

Cernik poured two cups of coffee and laid them on the table. He sat down on the edge of the divan. "We had meant to go over at Uhorska Ves. Now we shall have to go over somewhere nearer. Wait till I get a map." He rummaged in a locker, produced a large-scale map, spread it on the table. "We might go here, between Mikulov and Breclav; there's a good enough road there. We shall go tonight. I can't trust the tent-men. I shall send them ahead, somewhere up-country, say to Maravske-Budejovice. I shall send them ostensibly in the ordinary way, to set up in advance of us. They'll have the king-pole wagon and the tent."

"And the seating," Cheb reminded him.

"And the seating," Cernik agreed. "Now, if you would be willing to ambush them, that would cause another diversion and would be of value to me."

"That might be arranged," Cheb said. "And meantime you will let the wolves loose somewhere else?"

"Precisely," Cernik said. "Somewhere to the west, just far enough to pull off the police from the border. We shall create a formidable confusion. We shall in-form the police simultaneously that there are wild animals loose at points A, B, C, and D, and also, if you are agreeable, that there is a circus battle at point E. We shall bombard the police and the military with messages, and we shall frighten the public so that they, too, send in agitated messages. We shall give the

72

authorities time to make their initial dispositions, and then we shall cut the wires between Brno and the frontier, and between the frontier and Breclav and all points east. We shall then be in the vicinity of the border, and we shall go over by a simple stratagem or, if need be, by force. But there should be no need of force if the timing is right. The success of the entire plan depends on the timing of the cutting of the wires."

Cheb said, "There are many wires."

"I have twelve motor-cycles."

Cheb nodded approvingly. "I never could understand why you started that cycle act." He stroked the hair on his cheek, reflecting. "I am willing to arrange an ambush of your tent-men," he said at last. "But we shall have to make arrangements in detail. Where are the wolves to be freed? At what time? And the time and place of the ambush?"

They talked for ten minutes, fixing the details.

"Well," Cheb said finally, "I think that's everything. I hope you achieve it, Cernik. There is just one remaining thing. I shall have to wreck your caravan."

"I don't understand."

"We must fight," Cheb said. "It is the only way that I can justify my visit. Kaka will know I am here.

Your tent-men will know. The police also may learn of it. There must be no suspicion afterwards in the minds of any of them that I have come to warn you. We must fight, and you must throw me out of the caravan in front of them all."

"Very well," Cernik said. "But I must ask you to cause as little damage as possible. My wife——"

"I perfectly understand," Cheb said, getting to his feet. "We shall cause as little damage as is consistent with realism. Shall I commence?"

"If you please," Cernik said.

Cheb struck him immediately, and there was nothing artificial about the blow. It was a massive right swing with all the weight of Cheb's 220 pounds behind it, and it caught Cernik on the left cheek-bone and knocked him back over the edge of the divan on to the floor. As he got up, half-stunned, shaking his head, Cheb, trumpeting like a rogue elephant, picked up first one cup, then the other, and threw them against the door. He struck at Cernik again, but Cernik dodged and stumbled in close, thrusting his face for protection into the huge belly and at the same time bringing up his knee in an illegitimate but telling blow that levelled the score between them. They grappled and fell together, got up, wrestled, fell again. In a few seconds the caravan became a scene of

devastation as one after another of Mama's valued possessions crashed to debris on the floor.

As they rolled from under the table, Cernik contrived to scramble on to Cheb's back, and clung there like a limpet. He got a hand under Cheb's arm and on to the back of his neck, and for a long minute they held this pose, sweat breaking out on their faces as Cernik tried to enforce his half-nelson, taking the pressure on his wrist and using his arm as a lever to force Cheb's from its socket, while Cheb tried to break the grip with the muscles of his great neck, straining backwards with the deliberate intent of snapping Cernik's wrist-bone.

This was no mock battle. Neither would concede an inch, and some bone must surely have broken if a diversion had not come just then.

The door was thrust open, and Jaro's voice, calling Cernik's name, spilled into the caravan.

"Enough," Cernik panted. He got to his feet, flexing his fingers. His shirt and singlet were torn wide open at the chest, there was already a swelling on his cheek-bone, and his mouth was bleeding. Cheb also got up, shaking himself like some great shaggy bear. He had a red weal across his forehead where it had struck against the iron table-clamp. He said, "You'll suffer for this, Cernik."

"Get out," Cernik said. "Get out, and stay out." He saw the gaping spectators over Jaro's shoulder at the open door, and he raised his voice to ensure that everyone heard, "If ever you lay foot on my tober again, I'll kill you, Cheb. You or any of your men. I'll have you shot like the dogs you are."

"You haven't heard the last of this, Cernik," Cheb said. "Not by a long chalk." He brushed past Jaro, and as he went down the steps Cernik picked up his sombrero and threw it after him.

One of Cheb's men bent to pick it up, but Konradin said, "No." Konradin was standing with his rifle carelessly in his hands. He had been standing like that for the past half-hour, watching Cheb's men; and Cheb's men also had been watching him. Cheb glared at Konradin and himself picked up his hat. He jammed it on his head. "That's only a taste of what you can expect, Cernik," he said. "From now on it's war between you and me."

There was an ugly movement in the crowd, and Cernik said, "Let them be, men. We don't want trouble with the police. I'll settle this later in my own way."

Konradin said, "I shall help them into their car, Cernik."

"All right," Cernik said. "But no accidents."

Mama ran up the steps. "You're hurt, Cernik!"

"It's nothing."

"You're bleeding."

He touched his cheek. "It's nothing, Mama. Jaro, I want to speak to you."

"Daddy," Cara said, hugging him. "Oh, Daddy, I thought he'd killed you. Your poor eye! Mama, where's the first-aid box?"

"All right," Cernik said, raising his voice to the crowd. "All right now, break it up. Get back to work."

"Oh, my God!" Mama said. She began to wail: she had just seen the inside of the caravan. "Look at my lamp. Oh, *cruci*, look at the mess. . . ."

"Where are the bandages, Mama?"

"God knows where anything is. There's nothing left. They've even broken the stove. Look at my lovely picture that Maria gave me. . . ."

"I'll get bandages from Ma Bratislav, Daddy."

"I don't want bandages," Cernik said. "All I want is just some peace for the next half-hour." He looked ruefully at the mess in the caravan. "I'm sorry, Mama," he said gently. "But it's not so bad as it looks. You'll soon tidy it up. Cara'll help you."

"At your age!" Mama wailed. "Fighting like an animal. . . ."

"Maybe you'd better come over to my place, Cernik," Jaro said.

Cernik thought of all he had to do.

"Yes," he said, and he smiled at the fat man, exhilarated at the prospect of the action that lay ahead of them. "Jaromir, old capon, you and I have work to do."

5

BY MID-AFTERNOON THE PLAN WAS under way. A bellman had been round the village announcing that the afternoon and evening shows were cancelled. An advance agent had been sent on a wild-goose chase to Borovany to engage a tober that would never be used and to plaster the town with posters of a circus that would never be seen there. The Big Top and the assorted tents had been brought down, and all the poles, brackets, benches, chairs loaded on to the king-pole lorry. The beast wagons had been shuttered and bolted down, the prop trailer packed. Engines, tyres, lighting, pulling-bars had been checked; provisions taken on board; the tober cleared of refuse. The horses still grazed under the sycamore trees, and here and there an odd line of washing hung by a caravan door, but, by and large, mobilisation was complete and the circus stood buttoned up for the road. All day motor-cycles had roared out on reconnaisance and had been returning at intervals to bring Cernik news—news of the quality and gradients of the roads, of the lie of the land between Mikulov and Breclav, of the disposi-tions at the frontier post, of the telegraph wires between this town and that. Jaro's son brought facts gleaned from the public library in Brno. Fedor returned with a rough copy of a document in Breclav post-office. All day information poured in, and by four o'clock in the afternoon Cernik had every relevant fact at his finger-tips and had made his final arrangements.

With Jaro he walked round the decoy truck—a horse-box which was plastered with garish posters of ladies in tights and still more garish posters of nude women, stolen three months before from a theatre in Prague. Kubelik was up a ladder with paint-pot and brush, putting the finishing touches to a sign which read:

FOR MEN ONLY: THE MOST DARING SHOW EVER
PRESENTED

"All right," Kubelik said, grinning. "Eh, Cernik?"

"Looks all right to me," Cernik agreed.

There were some tent-men standing by, watching. "What's it in aid of?" one of them asked.

"It's a new show," Cernik said. He looked at his watch. "Why are you fellows still here? You, Houshka. You should have left five minutes ago."

"We haven't had no orders."

Cernik raised his eyebrows. He said, "Tell Zamek I want to see him. Right away."

"Cernik," Kubelik said, "if this little lot does not make our fortunes, so to speak"—and he cracked his favourite joke—"my name is not Josef Maravek."

"Very funny," Jaro said. "You should be a clown, Kubelik."

"You have not seen the point of it," Kubelik said. "I have told you before, but you have forgotten. My true name *is* Josef Maravek."

"You would be a riot in a false nose," Jaro said. "Cernik, do you think it would add to the effect of the notice if we had beneath in smaller letters: 'No man under 21 to be admitted'?"

"By all means," Cernik said. But his mind was elsewhere. He was watching Zamek, who had disengaged himself from a group of men playing cards by the lion-cage and who was now walking towards him. He was watching Zamek, and he was wondering.

Zamek was the gaffer of the tent-men. He was a Slovak in his middle thirties, a tall, thin man with a long, weather-beaten face and perplexed blue eyes. He was highly intelligent, although uneducated, and Cernik would have sworn that he was an honest man. He had been with the circus for the past two seasons, and he was the best foreman that Cernik had ever had.

83

"What's the matter, Zamek?" Cernik demanded. "You've had your orders, haven't you? You should be on the road."

Zamek looked from Cernik to Jaro to the ground. He traced a line on the grass with the toe of his boot.

"Well, what is it?" Cernik insisted.

"I've been thinking it over," Zamek said, in a slow, hesitant voice. "And I don't like it, Cernik."

"I'm surprised to hear that," Cernik said mildly. He was genuinely surprised, and he was also immediately on guard. He never acted the Boss. Every man on the pay-roll could speak his mind to him, but there were some things he did not expect ever to be challenged on, and circus movements was one of them. He looked hard at Zamek and saw that Zamek was sweating, and he grew very wary indeed. He said, "What don't you like, Zamek?"

"Well," Zamek said uneasily, "it's this change of plans. We've been going east for the past month, and I thought we were to go across Slovakia, and now all of a sudden there's this change of plan and we're doubling back to Borovany."

"You have a nerve, Zamek——" Jaro began.

"That's all right, Jaro," Cernik said. "The change of plans is none of your business, Zamek, but I don't mind telling you it has to do with Cheb. It concerns a little surprise I have up my sleeve for Mr. Cheb."

"Mebbe so," Zamek said. "But that's not all. You've given orders that Foster is to come with us. Foster's never come with us before. He's the horse-man. Why should he travel with us? Are you trying to get him out of the way? And why isn't Bratislav going on ahead as usual to mark out the tober? I've been thinking about it all day, Cernik, and I don't like it." He looked directly at Cernik, and there was no mistaking the challenge in his eyes. "There's something fishy going on, Cernik. I think you're up to something."

"But what business is it of yours?" Jaro demanded.

"It's my business all right," Zamek said stub-bornly.

"I think we had better discuss this in private, in the wagon," Cernik said, and he made a signal which included Jaro and Kubelik. "Come, Zamek." And all four of them went up the ramp into the wagon.

"Now, Zamek," Cernik said, and his voice was much brisker than it had been, "you have made some strange statements. Explain yourself, if you please."

"I don't want to make trouble for you," Zamek said. "You've always treated me decently. I know you're up to something, and I think it's to do with the

Countess. She's not worth running any risks for, Cernik. I wouldn't like to see you make a false move. I'm giving you fair warning."

"Go on speaking," Cernik said. He took a half-step forward, and Jaro and Kubelik also edged forward, forming a barrier between Zamek and the door. "Go on speaking, Zamek."

"I've said enough."

"You've said too much," Cernik said. "So you're the spy, are you? You're the one who's been informing on Madame?"

"I've only done my duty," Zamek said. He looked at the encircling ring of faces and squared his shoulders defiantly. "I've nothing against you, Cernik. But I'm not afraid of you either, not of any of you. I have more power than you think."

"You're a paid Government agent?" Cernik said.

"Not exactly."

"Just a busybody," Jaro said.

"No," Zamek said. "I am a loyal citizen, I don't need to be paid to do my duty. The revolution we have had is the greatest thing that has ever happened in Czechoslovakia. It is the duty of all citizens of the Republic to inform on the enemies of the Republic and to take whatever action may be necessary to safeguard the newly acquired liberties of the proletariat."

"For the love of God," Jaro said, "listen to the book talking!"

Zamek was watching Cernik. He saw the signal in Cernik's eyes, and he said in a high-pitched voice, "Don't start any rough stuff, Cernik. For your own sake——"

"Go on, Kubelik!" Cernik said.

"For your own sake, Cernik——"

The rest was unspoken. Kubelik's great hands went round Zamek's throat, there was a stifled scream, a moment's vicious flurry of action as when a terrier seizes on a rat.

"Knock him out," Cernik said.

Kubelik swung his right arm like a club; his fist crashed down on Zamek's skull; Zamek's knees sagged and gave way, and he slithered to the floor, falling crumpled and inert at Cernik's feet.

"So it was Zamek all the time!" Jaro said. "I'd never have thought of Zamek. I always liked him, trusted him. And all the time the swine was spying on us. . . ."

"An honest man," Cernik said. "A fanatic if you like, but an honest man. Tie him up, Kubelik. We took him to the right place when we took him to this wagon. There's enough rope here to tie up a regiment." He looked down at Zamek's body. He was

sorry about Zamek, and he was even a little sorry for Zamek. "Fanatics," he said. "They're the dangerous men, Jaro. They're the men you have to watch. An honest man like Zamek here, a fanatic, will cause more trouble than a thousand scoundrels."

Jaro smiled. "There are some who might call you a fanatic, Cernik."

"Well," Cernik said, "maybe I am."

Kubelik lifted a coil of rope from a barrel in the farthest corner. "What are you going to do with him, Cernik?" he asked.

"We'll have to take him with us, that's all we can do. Jaro, we've wasted enough time, we're behind now. Get the tent-men away. At once. Make old Klubal foreman. Tell him the road was marked this morning. There shouldn't be any difficulty."

"What shall I tell them about Zamek?"

"Just tell them he's sacked. Get them away quickly. And, Jaro——"

"Yes, Cernik."

"Make sure that Foster goes with them."

6

AT 16.16—SIXTEEN MINUTES BEHIND schedule—the king-pole lorry and trailer, with the tent-men on board, drew out of the tober, and a few minutes later Zamek, bound and gagged and entirely covered by sacking, was carried to the wardrobe van and deposited there under the watchful eye of Ma Bratislav. At 16.30 the wolf wagon pulled out. At 17.00 the motor-cyclists, having received a final briefing, were armed with synchronised watches, wire-cutters, and small explosives, and roared dramatically off on their missions.

And then the waiting began.

At 17.30 Cernik walked round the camp, checking that everything was ready and that everyone knew his job. He spoke to everyone, and he told the men that they might now give their womenfolk full details of the plan.

Returning to his caravan, he applied his mind to the matter of Zamek. It was all to the good that Zamek had revealed himself and was now out of harm's way. The problem of the spy had been gnawing at the back of his mind; it had worried him more than he had ever admitted, and it was a relief to know that he need no longer search men's eyes and probe their words for hidden meanings. The presence of a spy in the circus had been the greatest single threat to the security of the plan, and that threat was now removed.

He compared the plan to a giant engine, and the thought pleased him. It was ticking over nicely: he could detect no fault in it.

Mama was in one of her good moods. As he came into the caravan she was singing and she flashed him a smile over her shoulder. She was standing by the oven, preparing a meal, and, preoccupied though he was, he noted that she looked very young and pretty. Her hair was sleek and her face was made-up, and she was wearing a white blouse with a scarlet scarf knotted at the neck and a black silk skirt. The thought flashed through his mind that the clothes she was wearing were not very suitable for travelling. The other women, certainly, would be in dungarees and dust-caps. But he was glad that Mama was not like the other women.

He said, "Mama, I have something to tell you. We're going over the border tonight, into Austria."

"Austria!" Mama said, busy with the frying-pan. "But I thought we weren't allowed to leave the country."

"We're not allowed. We're breaking out."

She was immediately arrested in her movements. She said, "Is everybody going?"

"Yes," he said. "More or less everybody." He felt the pain that only Mama could give him. He knew that she was thinking of Rudolph. "The entire circus is going," he said.

She could not even leave it at that. She had to make it abundantly clear to him. "And the animals?"

"Yes," he said. "The animals too." He knew only too well what was in her mind. The lions. Those accursed cats. The cats exercised some terrible fascination over her. She had lain in his arms weeping in a storm of shame the night he had discharged the last trainer, Charles the Englishman. It wasn't the man, she said, it wasn't, it wasn't. She truly hadn't cared about Charles. It was the act and the whip and the smell of the cats. Oh, she couldn't explain it, she wouldn't ever be able to explain it, she didn't have the words, and she didn't have the knowledge of herself. But Cernik had partially understood, and his gentleness then had been more than she could bear, and she had clung to him in a frenzy of despair, begging him to help her and to save her from herself. And then Rudolph had come in Charles's place, and after a little it had all been as before, with the difference that Rudolph was a man of character. "All the animals are coming," Cernik said, "except the wolves. Everybody and everything except the tent-men and the Big Top stuff and the wolves. I'd have taken the tent-men too, only I couldn't trust them. We have a plan, Mama—I'll tell you about it—but it may not work; and if it doesn't, well, I might as well be frank with you, we may have to fight our way through."

"I'm not afraid, Cernik," Mama said, her eyes brilliant with excitement. "Austria, eh? I've never been in Austria, what's it like?"

"Much the same as here."

"Oh, I'm sure it's not. For one thing, there won't be so many policemen. Will we go to Vienna?"

"I expect so."

"When?"

"Oh, I don't know. Sooner or later."

Mama pirouetted back to the frying-pan. "I've always wanted to see Vienna," she said. "All those fine boulevards and the Danube and the Prater, and the beautiful women and the waltzes!" And she began to hum the *Tauberl-Walzer*. Cernik thought it likely that Vienna might be something of a disappointment to Mama, but he refrained from saying so. He had not been looking forward to telling Mama

94

of the plan. He had not known what her reaction would be, and he was greatly relieved to find her so pleased.

"When do we cross the border, Cernik?"

"Twenty-one hundred," he said. "This is the drill, Mama. There are to be diversions to the west to draw the guards from our part of the border. There'll be a great confusion. A circus battle, animals loose, people phoning from all over the district, reporting incidents, demanding protection. And then the wires are to be cut—all the wires—that's the motor-cyclists' job. And just after that, at 20.25, our advance party is to reach the border at the frontier post . . . here, I'll show you it on the map . . . between Mikulov and Breclav. . . ." He put his finger on the spot. "Just there. There are never more than a dozen men at this post, and I reckon maybe half of them might be drawn off by our diversions to the west. The advance party consists of the elephants and the lions and that wagon you saw Kubelik painting—the one with all the women plastered on it. Vina is to be in that wagon, and Kubelik and Konradin and Fedor. The guards will all come out to look at the elephants. . . . I sent the elephants off this morning: the advance party is to rendezvous them near the border. . . . They'll all be standing about, gaping. Rudolph'll show them the cats. They'll look at the posters on the wagon and ask what the show is. Rudolph will say that he can arrange for them to see it, provided they pay. I think that's a good touch, Mama—to make them pay. So they pay their money, and in they go, one at a time. There's a lot of laughing and screaming from Vina inside the wagon, and Konradin and Kubelik and Fedor will laugh too, but most of all it will be Vina's voice that the guards will hear. Only one is to be admitted at a time, and as he goes in he's knocked out, and Vina gives a little scream and laughs her head off. I think it'll work—it's the sort of simple trick that does work—and if it does, then we leave the wagon locked up at the frontier and the circus streams through."

Mama nodded in approval. "I don't see why it should be your sister, though. I could attract the men into the wagon a lot better than Vina could, you know I could, Cernik."

"They won't see her," Cernik said. "It's just her voice."

Mama put her hands on her hips. "And do you think, Jan Cernik, that your sister Vina has more allure in her voice than I have?"

"Of course not, Mama. You have more allure than any woman in the circus. Far more. It was just that

96

someone suggested Vina, and I agreed without thinking——"

"And who, I should like to know, suggested Vina in preference to me?"

"I think," Cernik lied, "that it was Jaro." In fact, it had been he himself who had insisted that Vina, as the most reliable of the women, should do this job, and he had had to bully Jaro into agreeing.

"Jaro, it would be Jaro!" Mama said. "That Jaro, he sometimes has the idea that he's running this circus. But fancy even Jaro thinking that his wife has more sex appeal than me! Goodness knows, I've nothing against Vina, Cernik, but really——"

"If you've nothing against her," Cernik said, "don't say it, Mama."

"All right," she said unexpectedly, and she smiled in genuine amusement. "I won't. But tell me, Cernik, what's going to happen if the trick doesn't work?"

"If the trick doesn't work we shoot our way through. The elephants will crash the barrier, and we go through by force. It shouldn't be difficult. There haven't been any incidents at this post, and they're not expecting trouble, and they can't call up rein⁄forcements. Konradin thinks he could do the whole job by himself if need be, but all the men will be armed, and there are openings concealed under the posters along the sides of the wagon that they can shoot through. We'll get out all right, Mama. And you'll like Austria, I'll guarantee that. We'll find winter quarters somewhere in the Tyrol, high up, and, who knows, we might go into Switzerland, or even to Italy. . . ."

Mama sighed happily. And then, suddenly, in that pleasurable and exciting moment, she remembered.

Her hand flew to her mouth in an ugly gesture of alarm, and her eyes swelled with fear.

"Cernik!" she said. "The tent-men!"

"They're on the way to Borovany. They're to be ambushed. . . ."

"No, no," Mama said. "It's Cara! Cara is with the tent-men."

"I don't understand."

"Cara, Cernik. She's with them. Oh, God help us! She asked me to cover up for her. Oh, Cernik, what have I done?"

Cernik felt cold and sluggish. He said slowly, "What are you speaking about, Mama? How could Cara be with the tent-men?"

"She went with Foster."

And then the whole story came tumbling out. For several weeks past, each time the circus had travelled by day, Cara had gone with Foster and the horses. Mama had known; had known, too, what Cernik's reaction would be, and she had deliberately helped Cara to deceive him.

"There's nothing wrong about it, Cernik," Mama said. "She's a good girl. And Foster. I don't care what you say about him. I know men. He's a good boy, Cernik. . . ." She faltered before his gaze and began to sob. "Don't hit me, Cernik," she begged. "How was I to know? . . . Oh Cara! . . ." And, unable to bear Cernik's eyes, she slumped down at the table and hid her face in her arms and wept bitterly.

Cernik tore the door open and ran.

He burst into Jaro's caravan, where Vina sat placidly knitting and Jaro stood by the window cleaning a rifle with a pull-through.

"Cara's gone with Foster," Cernik said. "With the tent-men. I'm going after her. I'm taking the Opel. Get the advance party off at 19.15. If I'm not back by 20.00, hook my caravan on to one of the lorries and leave without me."

They had no chance to speak. He was gone.

99

7

CERNIK DROVE WITH HIS FOOT HARD down on the accelerator. The Opel was an old car, first licensed in 1938. The body was scarred with makeshift patches, the windscreen cracked, the mudguards corroded. But the engine was sound. Cernik serviced it himself with meticulous care, and two days ago he had checked it over, cleaned the plugs, drained, flushed, and refilled the sump. He had confidence in the engine. He knew what it could do, and made it do it. He kept the speedometer needle flickering around the eighty kilo-metre mark, ruthlessly using the whole road and trusting to luck at the corners.

It was a fine evening. Ideal for the plan, he thought bitterly. Ideal for any project. The sun shone on the mountains, pricking colour from the bare peaks, mellowing the sombre pine-woods and lighting up the bright-tagged half-grown saplings of the foot-hills. Young linnets in flocks rose in alarm at Cernik's approach, and here and there peasants, at work in the fields, carting oats, hoeing turnips, flailing wheat, stopped work to stare after the roaring, bouncing car

and shake their heads in disapproval. Cernik saw nothing but the road.

He had been using the secondary road to the south of the Thaya. Now, at Satov, he crossed the river and bore north-west, along the broad Jemnice road that Bratislav, earlier that afternoon, had 'marked' for the king-pole lorry. He calculated that, allowing the king-pole lorry twenty kilometres per hour, he should overtake it in the region of Jemnice. The ambush didn't worry him. The ambush would not take place until 20.25, and he didn't give it a thought. What obsessed him was the need to get back to the tober to organise the circus's departure. Unless he overtook the king-pole lorry by 19.00 he could never get back to the tober by 20.00, and he might even be unable to reach the frontier-post in time to go through with the circus. Occasionally, in the dust at the roadside, he fancied he could see traces of the broad tyres of the lorry, and he told himself that the tracks were fresh, and drove furiously on. From time to time he cursed Foster with unfamiliar profanity, and leaned forward, gripping the wheel with all his strength concentrated in his fingers, trying to coax a few extra kilometres from the racing engine.

He caught up with the king-pole lorry earlier than he had dared hope. It was drawn up in an open parking-place by a wayside café, just beyond the village of Nova Trentlova. He looked at the time as he pulled the Opel up behind the lorry. 18.41.

Inside the café the tent-men were seated at a long deal table, talking boisterously, munching *pareks* and salami sandwiches, and swilling down red table-wine. As they became aware of Cernik standing straddle-legged in the doorway their conversation died away, and the silence spread until it included not only the circus party but also the workmen playing cards at a corner-table and the man and woman behind the counter. In the unnatural silence everyone watched Cernik.

"Come here, Cara," he said.

She got up immediately from her place at the bench beside Foster and came towards him, red and embarrassed, a shamefaced child. Old Klubal came bustling up between them, intent on justifying his new promotion. "See here, Cernik," he said guiltily, "we only been stopped five minutes. The boys wanted a break. The engine's a bit hot too. I thought there'd be no harm in stopping. But five minutes only, I said."

Cernik forced himself to consider what his reaction would have been if the circumstances had been normal. "Well, get them going," he said roughly. "Five minutes is long enough to stop on the road. Come on, Cara."

Klubal turned away, and began immediately to bluster at the tent-men.

Cara said in a low voice, "Don't make a scene, Daddy. Please don't make a scene in front of them all. I'm not coming back, and you can't make me. I won't be treated like a naughty child in front of all these men."

"This is something you don't understand," Cernik said. "I'll explain to you later. You're coming with me . . . *now*."

She said, "Well, can Foster come too?"

"No, he cannot."

"In that case," Cara said, "I shall stay, Daddy."

He moistened his lips. This was a difficulty he had not bargained for. He had been intent on overtaking Cara. It had not occurred to him that, having overtaken her, there could be any further trouble. If he had thought of it at all, he had thought merely that he would pack her into the car, and that would be that. He saw now that it was not to be so easy. He said, "I order you to come, Cara."

"Daddy," she said earnestly, "I've always done everything you ever asked me. But you are asking me to do something that disgraces me in front of the men.

Take Foster too. You could say that you want Foster for something to do with the horses. If you make it look as if you've come for Foster, I'll come with you. But I won't come without him. I won't have them thinking that you've chased after us just to bring me home—as if I'd done something wrong—or as if you thought I would."

Cernik looked at his daughter in perplexity. He saw that she was trembling, that there was the glitter of tears in the back of her eyes, but he saw also that she was set in her foolishness, determined to have her way. He was tempted to turn her upside down and spank her there and then and to carry her forcibly to the car, but, angry and urgent though he was, he had sense enough to realise that this was a delicate matter, not to be resolved by force. Cara had deceived him, but it had been a relatively innocent deception. She still trusted him and depended on him; her continuing faith, her confidence in him, their whole future relationship, might depend on his handling of this difficult situation. And he did not know how to handle it.

"Please, Daddy," she whispered. "Take Foster. Just to save my face. You can row me all you like afterwards. But please take him, please, Daddy!"

He felt time—valuable, essential time—slipping away from him. He began to sweat.

"Please, Daddy!"

"Foster," he said sharply, "you're wanted at the circus. The rosin-back. I came to get you. Look smart now!" And he took Cara by the arm and hustled her unceremoniously through the door.

Cara sat beside him in the front seat; Foster sat directly behind him, leaning forward, and every now and again he felt, with distaste, the boy's breath on his neck. He drove east as he had driven west, with nicely calculated recklessness.

There was little conversation.

Cara said, "Are you very angry with me, Daddy?"

And Cernik said, "Very. But we'll discuss that when we're alone."

Later, after a great deal of throat-clearing, Foster said, "What's wrong with the rosin-back, sir?"

And Cernik said, "Nothing."

Later still, as they were passing through Satov, the sight of a small child crossing the road aroused a sudden, disturbing thought in Cernik's mind, and he said, "Where was Kaka, Cara? I didn't see Kaka in the café."

"Kaka wasn't with us, Daddy."

Cernik said sharply, "Didn't he leave the circus in the king-pole wagon?"

106

"No. At least I didn't see him. Did you?" she asked Foster.

"What's that?" Foster begged, edging forward like a dog.

"Kaka," Cara said. "He wasn't with us, was he?"

"No," Foster said. "No, sir, I haven't seen that dwarf all day."

Cernik sucked his lips into a thin tight line. Kaka always travelled with the tent-men. Why wasn't he with the tent-men now? Where could he be? What mischief was he up to? . . . He took a hand off the steering-wheel, slipped a cigarette into the corner of his mouth, and lighted it adroitly. If he lived through this day he would not readily forget it. Only a few hours ago it had seemed that nothing could go wrong. Now it seemed that nothing would go right. He glanced at his watch. It was tempting Fate to entertain the thought. Nevertheless, he entertained it; at least he was making good time.

8

THERE WERE NO FLAGS OUT FOR
Cernik when he drove on to the tober twenty
minutes before the time scheduled for the
circus's departure. No congratulations. No one even
mentioned that he or she was glad to see Cernik back.
Nevertheless, it was a triumphant return. All the circus folk converged on the car as he drew it up by his
caravan, and he saw his welcome on their faces and
felt their unspoken relief. He got out and stretched himself, noting that the horses were now in the horse-
boxes and that all the trailers were hooked to their
lorries.

"Bratislav," he said, "get me tied up to the Opel.
Jaro, I want to speak to you." And he walked a few
yards away from the crowd.

"It's Kaka," he said.

"I've been waiting to speak to you about Kaka,"
Jaro said. "He's here, Cernik. I found him just after
you left."

"Where?"

"With Madame. He's been with her all day."

"Madame again!" Cernik said. "Why didn't he
go with the tent-men?"

"Says he was scared. After that business with the apes' food. Appears some of the tent-men thought he got off too light and they told him what they were going to do to him. They were going to give him the thumb."

It was an old tenting torture, and Cernik could understand Kaka's fear. He nodded, partially satisfied. "Where is he now?"

"In Madame's caravan, hiding behind her skirts. He's singing very low. Wants to apologise to everybody."

"He's still scared, eh?"

"Scared stiff," Jaro said. "What are we to do with him, Cernik?"

"Leave him," Cernik said. "He's safer with Madame than wandering around the countryside. We've pulled his teeth. Just let him be."

"Cernik," Mama called from the door of the caravan, "do you want to eat?"

He had not eaten since midday, and he knew that he ought to be hungry, but the thought of food sickened him. "Coffee," he said. "Just some coffee. What's the matter, Jaro? You look about as gay as Grimaldi."

"It's Vina," Jaro said. "They'll have picked up the elephants by now. They must be very near the frontier. I can't help worrying about her, Cernik."

Cernik nodded. He also was anxious, and he knew that if Mama had been in the decoy wagon his anxiety would have been almost unbearable. This was no time for facile optimism. He clapped Jaro on the shoulder. "I'm going to have some coffee before we hit the road. Come and have a cup with me. But first, while I'm getting cleaned up, you might tell Cara the drill. She doesn't know anything about it yet. Give her the details."

"She's to help Ma Bratislav with the ammunition, isn't she?"

"That's right," Cernik said. "See you later." And he turned away, pulling at the tired flesh round his jaw, and stepped into his caravan.

"I *am* sorry, Cernik," Mama said. "Truly sorry."

"No harm done," said Cernik, wrestling with his shirt.

"I didn't mean to deceive you; I truly didn't, Cernik. It was just that she wanted so much to go, you see, and I didn't think there was any harm in it."

"All right, Mama," Cernik said. "Forget it."

He washed to the waist, soaping the sweat under his arms, exulting in the shock of the cold water. "First thing I'm going to do in Austria is sleep," he said. "I'm going to sleep for twenty-four solid hours. How's that coffee, Mama?"

"Just on the boil."

He was towelling himself vigorously when there was a knock on the door. He said, "Come in, Jaro," and Foster stepped into the caravan, closing the door carefully behind him.

"I just heard where we're going," Foster said. "I had to speak to you." He stood inside the open door, long-legged and gangling and awkward. Cernik stopped towelling himself and looked at the boy's long, earnest face. Horseman! he thought. Looks like one of his own foals. He began to towel himself again. "So what?" he demanded.

Foster looked from Cernik to Mama, searching for an ally. "I can't come," he blurted out. "I can't leave the country. Listen, this is how it is. I'm a deserter."

Cernik's eyes were cold.

"I'm not an ordinary deserter. I didn't desert during the war. It was after. Listen, Mr. Cernik, you got to believe me. I was nearly due to go home."

"You were in the U.S. Army?" Cernik said.

"That's right, I was in the infantry. I would never have deserted if the war hadn't been over. Listen, please believe me, Mr. Cernik. I couldn't go home. I was married, you see. And my wife, I'd had a letter from her. Listen, I was a farm-boy at home; that's how I know about horses. And I got married before

I went overseas. I married my boss's daughter. I was only a kid, and so was she. We only had three weeks, that was all, and then I was sent overseas. And then I got this letter from her, saying she was divorcing me; she was sorry and all that, she wanted to marry some other fellow, fellow I never heard of. She said it wouldn't make no difference to her old man; she said my old job was waiting for me on the farm. But I couldn't go home. Folks being sorry for me, same folks that told me I was a fool to marry her—and they were right. Going back to my old job on the farm, that was a helluva thing for her to say, and her and her new husband there! Folks watchin' me to see how I was takin' it, and being sorry for me, and talkin' about me and mebbe laughin' at me a little too, how I was the green boy thought I was settin' myself up pretty for life. Mr. Cernik, Mrs. Cernikova, you got to see it, I couldn't go home. And so I walked out. Tech-nically, I'm a deserter. But that's not the way I see it. I've never done anything I have to be ashamed of, I've never done any harm to any mortal living person. But I can't go into Austria. If I cross the border, they'll arrest me, I'll be sent home, sent to prison for mebbe a year, mebbe two years. You got to believe me, Mr. Cernik; that's the truth I been tellin' you, the whole truth, and that's why I can't come with you."

"I believe you, Foster," Cernik said. He pulled on his shirt and began to button it up. He believed every word the boy had spoken. Sincerity shone out of him. It was as Mama had said. He was a good boy; a good, honest boy whose life, like so many thousands of others, had been knocked out of joint by the war. Now that Foster could no longer be a menace to Cara's happiness, Cernik looked at him for the first time with unprejudiced eyes, and liked what he saw. He said, "I'm sorry you can't come with us, Foster," and it was almost—although not quite—true. "I understand the position. And now you want your wages, that's it, isn't it?"

"Not exactly," Foster said. He shifted his weight gawkishly from one foot to the other. "Listen," he said. "Oh, darn it, ain't no way to say it but to tell you right out. I'm here to ask your permission to ask Cara to marry me."

Cernik stiffened.

"You . . . want to ask Cara to marry you?"

"That's right, sir."

"You must be mad in the head," Cernik said.

"No, listen, please listen to me, Mr. Cernik. I told you I was married before. I told you the truth about that, don't hold it against me. I was only a kid, I didn't know what I was doing. This is different, the way Cara and I feel. This is for keeps. I'll be a good husband to her, Mr. Cernik, I swear I will. . . ."

As Foster talked Cernik pulled out his note-case, selected three notes, and laid them on the table. His voice cut sharply through Foster's protestations:

"There's your money. Take it, and get out!"

"You don't understand," Foster said. "Oh, golly, I been tryin' to do it the proper way, like I want it to be done. I been askin' you. Now I got to tell you. If you're going into Austria, Cara's stayin' with me."

Cernik said, with dangerous calm, "I see. Have you consulted Cara?"

"I have, sir. She knows the whole story, and she's going to stay with me. We'll get married, get jobs with some other circus. . . ."

"Has it occurred to you," Cernik said, "that Cara cannot marry without my consent?"

"I don't see why not."

"She's not old enough, that's why not."

"She's a woman," Foster argued. "She's twenty."

"She is seventeen."

"She's twenty," Foster said. He appealed desperately to Mama. "She told me she was twenty."

"She's only seventeen, Foster," Mama said.

"And as such," Cernik said, "she cannot, and will not, marry anybody."

114

Foster had gone very red in the face. He looked from Cernik to Mama in a dismay that, in other circumstances, might have seemed comical. "I wish she hadn't told me. . . . Just the same," he said, "she'll stay with me."

"Mama," Cernik said, "get Cara!"

Mama nodded and went to the door.

"I wish you'd listen to me, Mr. Cernik. . . ."

And then Mama gave a little scream and backed away from the door, and Cernik saw that Zamek stood there, a revolver in his hand, his eyes no longer bewildered but burning with a fanatical purpose. He said, "Back against the table, all of you!"

Foster, his reflexes conditioned by American films, had already put his hands up. Now, obeying a jerk of the revolver, Mama also raised her hands. Cernik, fingers soft with fear, fastened the last button on his shirt. He said, "What nonsense is this, Zamek?"

"No nonsense, Cernik," Zamek said, "and you know it. I've found out what you meant to do, and I thank God that I've found out in time to stop you."

"I thought God was a bourgeois capitalist conception," Cernik said, using words as a shield—the first words that came into his head. "I'm surprised to hear such a term on your lips. How did you get free?"

He remembered Kaka. "That accursed dwarf, I suppose."

"Never mind how I got free," Zamek said. "Cernik, listen to me, you've been misguided, you're making a mistake—a tragic mistake. This government is ours. It belongs to us. It's made up of people like you and me. I've been with you for two years, I know you, Cernik. You're no traitor. But this is the act of a traitor, don't you see? Cernik, you've been misled, gulled by propaganda. Now listen, you've got to countermand your orders. I'll see to it you get a fair trial. I'll speak for you myself. . . . Don't move, Foster! One more move like that, and I'll put a bullet in you! . . . I'm going to open the door, Cernik, and you're going to call for Jaro, tell him the escape's off, tell him to send someone to recall the advance party. You were crazy to think you could ever do this thing. Now don't argue, Cernik. You've no choice. Co-operate with me, and I'll do all I can to help you. Refuse, and I have to kill you. Now I'm going to open the door. You call Jaro. . . ."

Cernik said, "Listen, Zamek, you and I have always got on well together. I respect you, and I think you respect me. We have a different point of view. I reckon you're entitled to your point of view. Surely I'm entitled to mine. You don't want to kill me,

Zamek. You're not a murderer, you're an honest man. Go your way, and let me go mine."

"No use, Cernik," Zamek said. "You're talking crazy. There's only one true belief, my belief, our Czechoslovak belief. You're acting like a traitor. You're a traitor to the cause, Cernik. It's my duty to stop you."

"But you can't stop me," Cernik argued. He was playing desperately for time. At any moment Jaro should arrive for his coffee, and the moment of Jaro's arrival would be the moment for action. "You can't stop the circus going through now. You may kill me, but that won't stop the circus; and it won't do you any good, Zamek, or your cause either, because the sound of your shot will bring every man on the tober here, and they'll kill you, Zamek. They'll kill you just as surely as you will have killed me."

"I'm not afraid to die, Cernik. You can't frighten me. If I have to die, I shall die gladly. I shall have done my duty." He pulled open the door, simul⁄ taneously flattening himself against the wall. "Call for Jaro, Cernik," he said. "Order him to cancel all these crazy plans to escape."

"I shall not call for Jaro," Cernik said. He had begun to sweat. He felt sweat trickling, like columns of lice, down his chest, down his flanks, down his

arms into his hands. "I shall never give that order," he said.

Zamek cocked his wrist, levelling the revolver so that it pointed at Cernik's head. Zamek was sweating too. "Last chance, Cernik. Call Jaro!"

"I shall never call him."

He saw Zamek's burning eyes and the little deadly dark hole through which his death would travel faster than sound. He saw the two blazing orbs and dull orb, and saw them only. They loomed and fixed him. There was nothing else in his field of vision. There was nothing else, and now never could be anything beyond this terrible triangle. As from a long way off he heard a voice, Zamek's, say, "It's my duty," and another voice, a strange voice, his own perhaps: "It won't do you any good, Zamek."

Mama, watching Zamek's trigger finger, screamed suddenly, and Foster moved, flinging himself forward at Zamek in an acrobatic leap that carried him over an intervening chair. He flew through the air, and the clawing fingers of his hand at the full stretch of his arm touched the muzzle of the revolver at the very moment of explosion.

And then, for Cernik, there was only a fearful confusion.

There were more explosions. There were voices.

Voices everywhere. Voices and faces. There was Mama, there was Cara, there was Jaro, Bratislav, Foster. There was blood. Blood in his hand. He turned his wrist and spilled it on the floor. Blood in his mouth.

Mama had become Cara, had become his old mother, had become Cara again. Cara was crying. He felt her tears on his face. "Don't cry, Cara," he wanted to say.

"Daddy, Daddy," she was saying . . . why did she have to shout so? . . . "I can't leave him now, I can't ever leave him. You see that, Foster, don't you!"

Of course he saw. He tried to say, "I'm not going to leave you, Cara." But he didn't know whether he said it or not. He wished they wouldn't all shout so. . . . Foster, Cara, Jaro. . . .

Mama was sponging him now. Mama was crying too. Silly Mama. With her little cool tickling hands. And Foster's face was stuck on top of Mama's head, grotesquely, and Foster was saying, "All right, I'll drive the Opel. Listen, Cernik. I'll give myself up. You need every man now. All right, I'll drive the Opel. I'll get a year, mebbe two, but I'll come back. She'll wait for me. I'm coming back for her, Cernik, if I have to swim."

"That's right," he said. Or thought he said. "You

drive the Opel, Foster." A good boy, Foster, he thought. A good, honest boy.

Jaro said, "Everybody out!" Jaro was hurting him. "Scream if you want to," Jaro said. He tried to say, "Go to hell," but was almost sure afterwards that he hadn't said it. Mama put something in his mouth, something that wasn't meant to go in anybody's mouth, a stocking or a rolled⁄up bandage. "Bite on that," somebody shouted. "Bite on that, on that, on that. . . ."

The pain was too much, and the smell strange and horrible, and he was being suffocated. He shouted, "I want to get away from it all", or would have shouted if it hadn't been for the thing in his mouth, and his wish was immediately granted and he faded away.

And then when he came back from being a long way off, Mama was with him, only Mama, thank God, smoothing his hair back from his forehead, moistening his lips with water, whispering of her love and her need of him, making wild beautiful promises that he knew very well she could never keep.

"*Drahousku*, oh *drahousku*, darling," she kept saying, and her tears fell softly on him.

He wanted to tell her not to cry, that it was all right, that everything was all right, he was going on a long journey with his golden girl, and he was very, very

happy. But he was too tired to speak. All he could do was drop his hand on to her sleek bowed head, and then he slipped away again.

He was still sleeping when the circus crossed the frontier. It crossed at 21.00 hours, on schedule and without incident, and, leaving behind it a horse-box plastered with posters of nude women, streamed proudly into Austria.

9

THE ADVENTURE OF THE CIRCUS
Cernik did not go unnoticed. There were posters in the streets of the world next day, and
banner headings in a thousand newspapers. Cernik
was pleased with the press notices. He had them sent
to him from all over Europe, from Asia, from the
Americas, and he got Mama to paste them in a series
of scrapbooks.

During his convalescence he made a hobby of
studying these clippings, and he learned some of
them by heart. He particularly liked the leading
article in the *Continental Daily Mail* in which his feat
of taking elephants through the Iron Curtain was
compared to that of putting camels through the eye of
a needle. But his favourite extract was from *Pravda,*
and he liked to recite it in full.

INTERNATIONAL INCIDENT

"It is reported from Prague that last night the
Circus Cernik, *en route* in thick fog to Borovany,
inadvertently crossed the frontier into Austria
between Mikulov and Breclav. When the error
was discovered the circus immediately turned

about, but Austrian guards refused to permit its return and opened fire on the defenceless caravan-folk, killing T. Zamek, foreman in charge of tents, and wounding others.

"The Czechoslovakian Government has sent a strongly-worded note to the Austrian Government, demanding the immediate return of the circus and full reparations. It has also instructed its ambassador in Vienna to make similar strong representations to the occupying powers.

"Further details of the outrage are still awaited, but it is already clear that this is the most flagrant case yet reported of the persistent kidnapping of Czechoslovakian nationals by agents of the Western powers. Tass reports that Jan Cernik, proprietor of the Circus Cernik, was a staunch supporter of the new Republic, and a leading member of the Czechoslovak Communist Party."

THE END

For regular
early information
about

FORTHCOMING
NOVELS

send a postcard giving

your name and address in

block capitals to:

The Fiction Editor:

HODDER & STOUGHTON LTD.

1, St. Paul's House

Warwick Square

London, E.C.4